Animal Behavior Investigations

ANIMAL SOCIETIES

By Tracie Santos

Rourke Educational Media
A Division of Carson Dellosa Education

ROURKE'S
SCHOOL to HOME
CONNECTIONS
BEFORE AND DURING READING ACTIVITIES

Before Reading: *Building Background Knowledge and Vocabulary*

Building background knowledge can help children process new information and build upon what they already know. Before reading a book, it is important to tap into what children already know about the topic. This will help them develop their vocabulary and increase their reading comprehension.

Questions and Activities to Build Background Knowledge:

1. Look at the front cover of the book and read the title. What do you think this book will be about?
2. What do you already know about this topic?
3. Take a book walk and skim the pages. Look at the table of contents, photographs, captions, and bold words. Did these text features give you any information or predictions about what you will read in this book?

Vocabulary: *Vocabulary Is Key to Reading Comprehension*

Use the following directions to prompt a conversation about each word.

- Read the vocabulary words.
- What comes to mind when you see each word?
- What do you think each word means?

Vocabulary Words:

- *hierarchy*
- *incubate*
- *interact*
- *observed*
- *predators*
- *societies*
- *solitary*
- *territory*

During Reading: *Reading for Meaning and Understanding*

To achieve deep comprehension of a book, children are encouraged to use close reading strategies. During reading, it is important to have children stop and make connections. These connections result in deeper analysis and understanding of a book.

Close Reading a Text

During reading, have children stop and talk about the following:

- Any confusing parts
- Any unknown words
- Text to text, text to self, text to world connections
- The main idea in each chapter or heading

Encourage children to use context clues to determine the meaning of any unknown words. These strategies will help children learn to analyze the text more thoroughly as they read.

When you are finished reading this book, turn to the next-to-last page for **Text-Dependent Questions** and an **Extension Activity**.

Table of Contents

Case Study: What Brings You Here?

The scientists have been watching the African elephants for weeks. They have tracked where the elephants have been moving. Sometimes an elephant will wander away from an area and return later. The scientists have noticed something strange, though: many of the same elephants return to the same place. Why do you think the elephants keep returning?

African Elephants

Two adult female elephants, named Echo and Emily, **interact** with each other frequently. The scientists find out that both Echo and Emily are going back to the same place at night. There are several young elephant calves there too. What is happening here? As you learn more about animal **societies**, you can help the scientists solve this mystery.

Better Together

Animals interact with each other in different ways. Some animals are mostly **solitary**. They only come together to eat or find a mate. Others spend their whole lives in a group. Some animals only interact a little bit within a group. Other animals do specific things in their group, such as performing a job for the rest of the animals around them. Some groups are big, and some are small. Not all animal societies are alike.

Gray Wolves

Honey Bees

Living in a society can help animals. It can make it easier for them to find food and protect themselves from predators. Some societies even help animals raise each other's young. Not all interactions are positive, though. Some animals fight within their group to establish who is in charge.

Leafcutter Ants

Being Social

Animal groups are sometimes organized around a hierarchy. Leafcutter ants from the same nest can have different jobs. Some defend the group. Others protect young ants or clean the nest. All of the ants protect the queen.

Gray wolves can have a complicated hierarchy. Some wolves can make decisions for the entire pack. Others make few or no decisions. They all protect their pack if they find other wolves in their territory.

Who's the Boss?

Gray wolves have many ways to show who is in charge. They sometimes growl at or bite another wolf who is behaving badly. If they want to play instead, they might rest their chest on the ground and lower their head. This is called a *play bow*.

Living in a group allows animals a greater level of safety. Vulturine guineafowl (VUL-chur-een GIHN-ee-fowl) live together during part of the year. They form small groups with just a few members. They meet up with other groups to drink water. Predators are more likely to attack a small group of birds instead of a large one.

Common guillemots (GILL-uh-mots) also stay safe in numbers. They make nests very close to one another. They get so close that the warmth from other birds helps incubate the eggs!

Some animal societies even help their members learn. African elephants can live in family groups with many generations. The groups usually have a few adults and young elephants. The young learn how to eat, drink, stay safe, and play by watching older elephants. The group may spread apart during the day, but they join back together at night.

Leaving Home

Scientists once thought that male African elephants left their family group when they were around 15 years old. Scientists now know that this is not always the case. Many male African elephants live with other males or even join other family groups throughout their lives.

Even fish can learn! Scientists have observed young guppies learning from older guppies. They watch the older fish find food and swim through paths. They copy what the older fish are doing and learn new things.

A Family Affair

Think about the elephants from the case study. What do you think their society is like? Do you know what's happening?

The elephants the scientists studied are living in a family group. This family group helps the elephants survive. The members of the group go to different places during the day. They stay together at night. The young elephants can learn from the older ones in their family group. Now the scientists understand why the elephants were together.

To learn more about the case study and scientists in this book, search online for "Amboseli Elephant Research Project" and "Dr. Cynthia Moss."

Get Creative! Animal Extension Activity

Think about the different kinds of animal societies and groups around you. How do the animals and people around you behave? Research other animal societies and choose one. Design a study that could help you learn more about it.

When designing your study, think about the following things:

1. What animal society or group are you studying?
2. What information about the society would you like to find out about?
3. How do you think living in this society helps the animals?
4. How could you test whether your guess was correct?

Design your study. Make sure it is safe for living things. Write a plan for your study and share it with a friend.

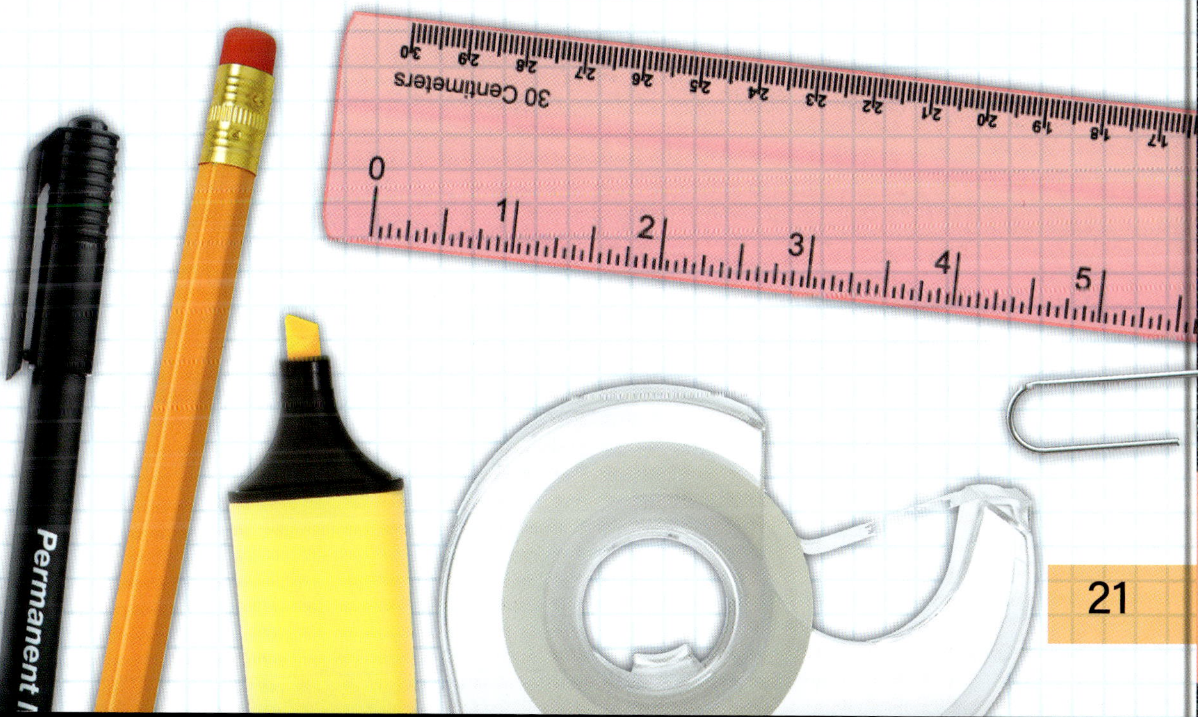

Glossary

hierarchy (HYE-ur-ahr-kee): an arrangement in which people, animals, or things have different ranks or levels of importance

incubate (ING-kyuh-bate): to keep eggs warm before they hatch

interact (in-tur-AKT): to talk, play, or otherwise share information and contact with another

observed (uhb-ZURVD): noticed and perceived someone or something

predators (PRED-uh-turz): animals that live by hunting other animals for food

societies (suh-SYE-i-teez): a group of living things with common goals

solitary (SAH-li-ter-ee): not requiring, or without the companionship of, others

territory (TER-i-tor-ee): the area under control of someone or something in charge

Index

Text-Dependent Questions

1. What are four ways that living in groups helps animals survive?
2. Why did the African elephants in the case study all return to the same place?
3. Would you call a gray wolf society simple or complicated, and why?
4. What is special about common guillemot nests?
5. Why do we say that not all animal group interactions are positive?

Further Reading

Dutcher, Jim and Jamie. *Running with Wolves* , National Geographic Kids, 2019.

Parker, Steve. *Fish*, DK Children, 2005.

Simon, Seymour. *Elephants*, HarperCollins, 2018.

About the Author

Tracie Santos has loved animals since she was very young. She has worked in zoos and aquariums and studied many amazing animal behaviors. She lives in Columbus, Ohio, and loves learning about naked mole rat societies.

"Cyrus" and "Jeff"

www.rourkeeducationalmedia.com

PHOTO CREDIT: Cover ©Jane Rix, ©Cezary Wojtkowski, ©Soho A Studio; back cover ©panpilai paipa; p4 ©Elephant Voices; p5 ©Sun_Shine, ©Michael Sheehan; p6 ©imageBROKER.com; p7 ©Leigh Gregg; p8 ©Marc Stephan, ©Kuttelvaserova Stuchelova, ©32 Pixels; p9 ©AB Photographie, ©RUKSUTAKARN; p10 ©Bildagentur Zoonar GmbH; p11 ©maxontravel, ©Pedro Turrini Neto, ©hansen.matthew.d, ©32 Pixels; p12 ©imv; p13 ©Raphael Rivest, ©Nicholette Wollentin; p13 ©32 Pixels; p14 ©Ralph H. Bendjebar; p15 ©David Havel; p16 ©ZambeziShark, ©32 Pixels; p17 ©slowmotiongli, ©Aleron Val, ©32 Pixels; p18 ©Bildagentus Zoonar GmbH; p19 ©Katja Forster; p21 ©BonD80, ©Boltenkoff, ©MyImages, ©Hurst Photo, ©Frame Art, ©32 Pixels; p24 ©Taryn Lindsey

Edited by: Tracie Santos
Cover and interior layout by: Tammy Ortner

Library of Congress PCN Data

Animal Societies / Tracie Santos
(Animal Behavior Investigations)
ISBN 978-1-73164-939-3 (hard cover)(alk. paper)
ISBN 978-1-73164-887-7 (soft cover)
ISBN 978-1-73164-991-1 (e-Book)
ISBN 978-1-73165-043-6 (ePub)
Library of Congress Control Number: 2021935268

Rourke Educational Media
Printed in the United States of America
01-1872111937